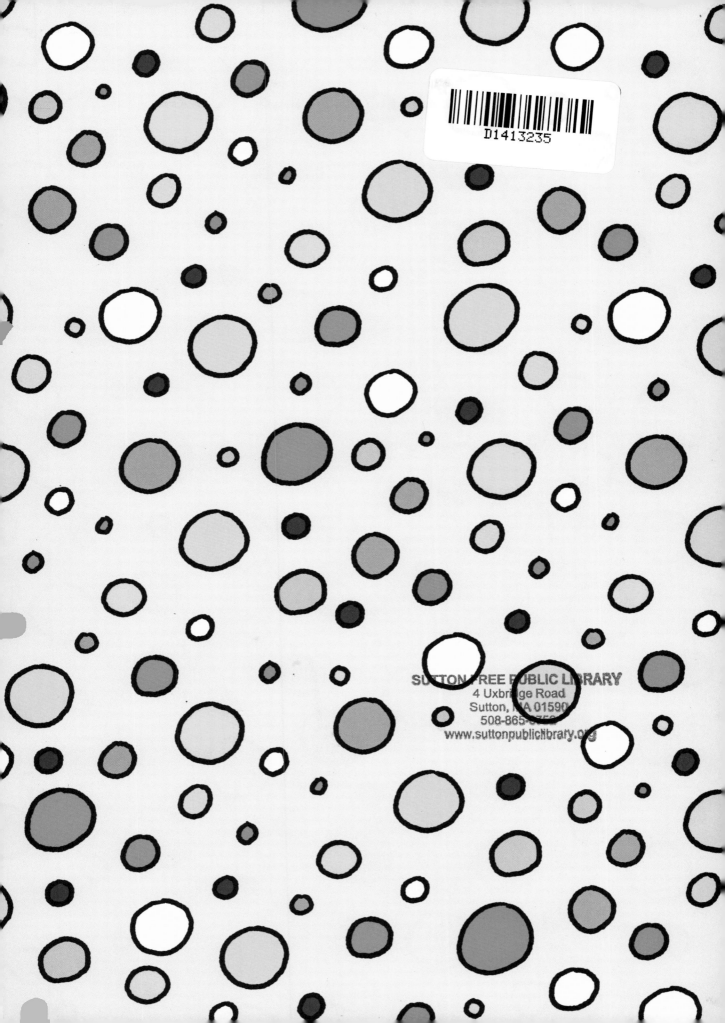

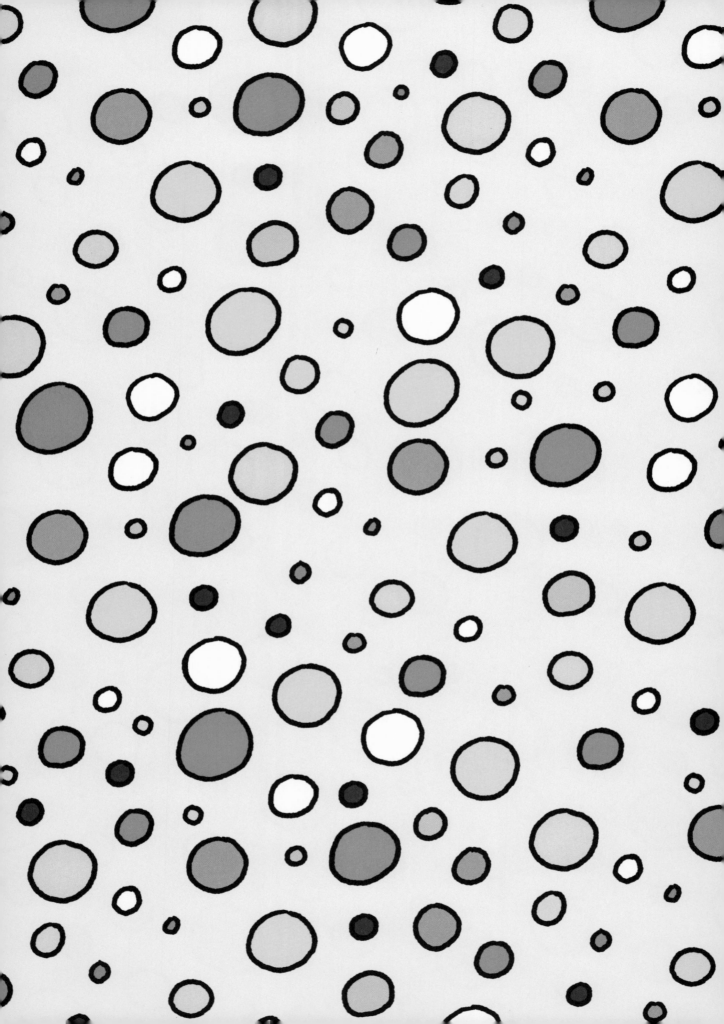

EVERYBODY!
You, Me & Us

ELISE GRAVEL

SCHOLASTIC PRESS
New York

EVERYBODY

is unique and different.

But we are more
similar than we think.

EVERYBODY

has fears.

EVERYBODY

has moments of joy...

and moments
of sadness.

and everybody can learn
from them.

EVERYBODY

wants friends...

and everybody
can be a friend.

EVERYBODY

gets angry sometimes.

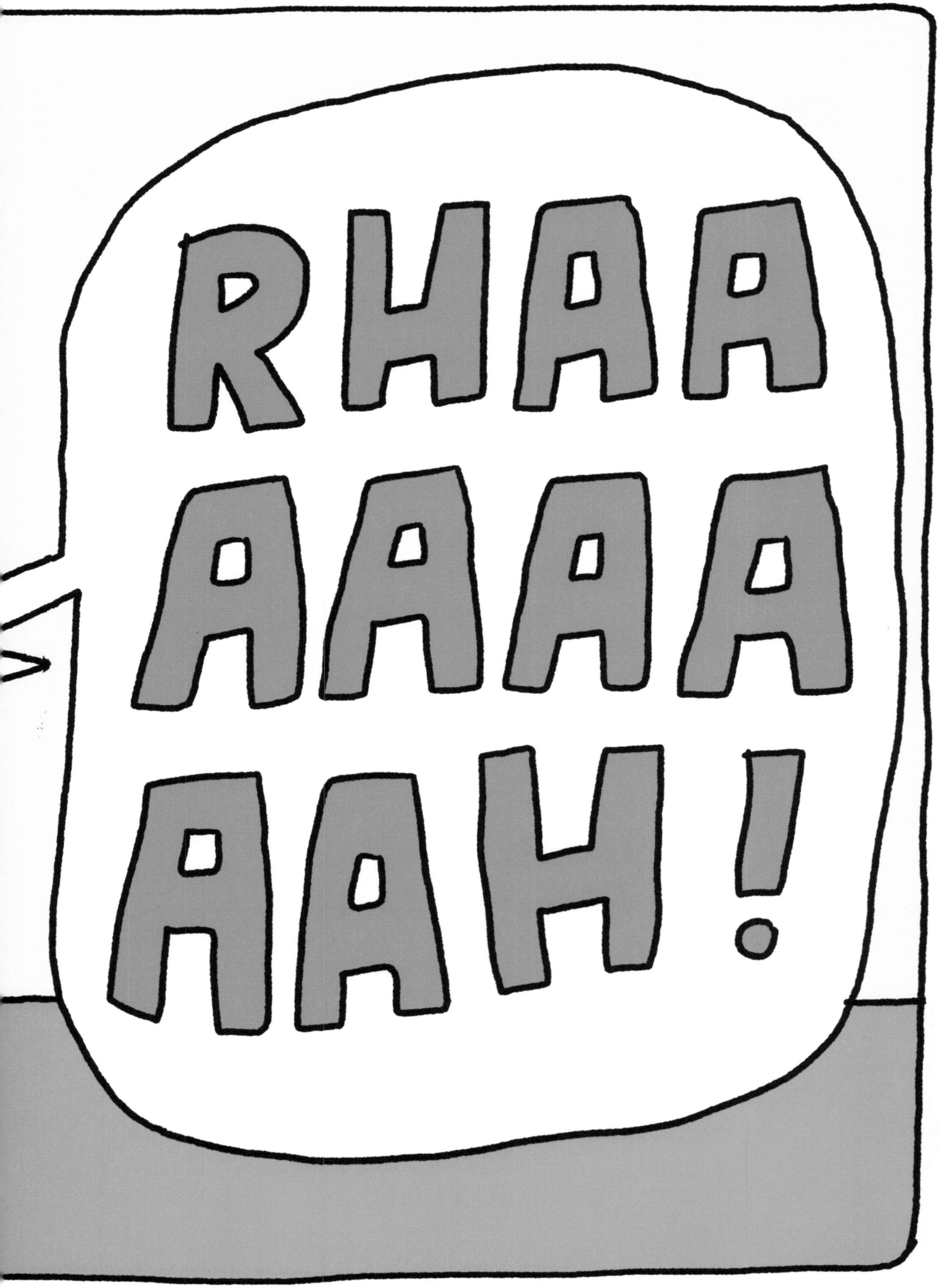
RHAAAAAAAAH!

EVERYBODY

goes to the bathroom.

and everybody likes
to feel useful.

BLAH BLAH.
BLAH BLAH!
BLAH BLAH.
BLAH
BLAH BLAH.
BLAH BLAH.
BLA
BLAH BLAH!
BLAH!

EVERYBODY

gets embarrassed.

EVERYBODY

feels tired from time to time...

and everybody needs to take care of themselves.

EVERYBODY

gets discouraged
once in a while.

EVERYBODY
struggles sometimes.

EVERYBODY

has hopes and dreams.

EVERYBODY

has ideas.

EVERYBODY

needs to be loved...

and accepted
just as they are.

EVERYBODY
deserves to be treated with
RESPECT.

We are each unique,
but we have so much
in common.

We are all

HUMAN.

To Monique and Chantale.

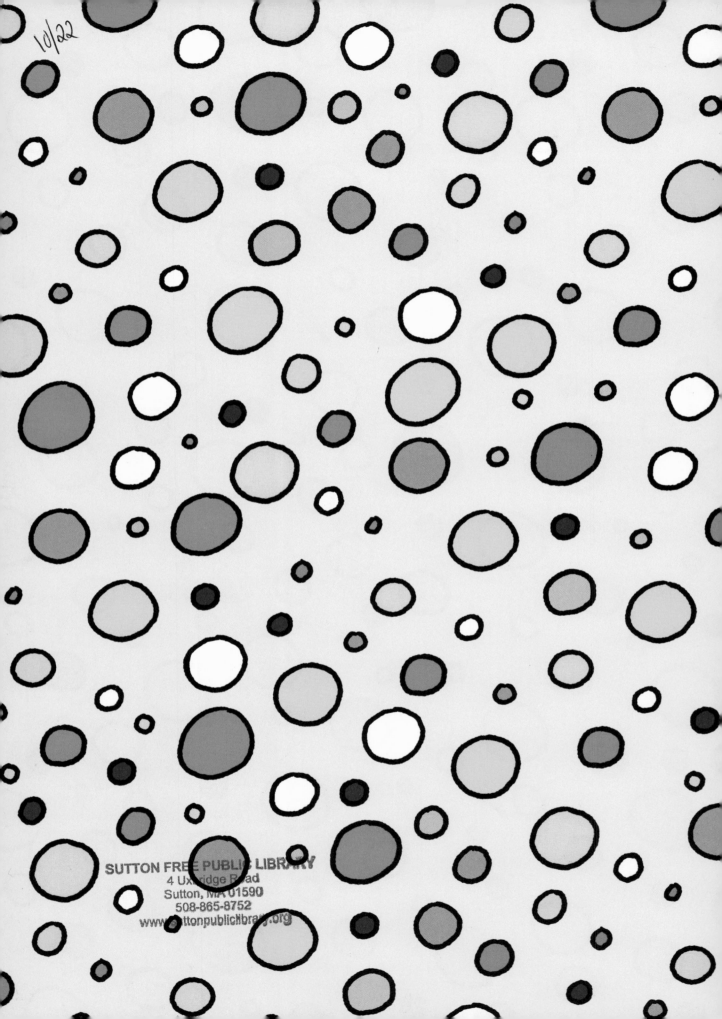